Cold Little Duck, Duck, Duck

by **Lisa Westberg Peters**

Pictures by **Sam Williams**

Greenwillow Books • *An Imprint of HarperCollinsPublishers*

Pencil and watercolors were used for the full-color art.
The text type is Bauer Bodoni Black BT.

Cold Little Duck, Duck, Duck
Text copyright © 2000 by Lisa Westberg Peters Illustrations copyright © 2000 by Sam Williams.
Printed in Mexico . All rights reserved.
http://www.harperchildrens.com

Library of Congress Cataloging-in-Publication Data
Peters, Lisa Westberg.
Cold little duck, duck, duck / by Lisa Westberg Peters ; pictures by Sam Williams.
p.   cm.   "Greenwillow Books."
Summary: Early one spring a little duck arrives at her pond and finds it still frozen, but not for long.
ISBN 0-688-16178-2 (trade).   ISBN 0-688-16179-0 (lib. bdg.)
[1. Ducks—Fiction.   2. Spring—Fiction.   3. Stories in rhyme.]
I. Williams, Sam, ill.   II. Title.   PZ8.3.P443Co   2000   [E]—dc21   99-29880   CIP

1 2 3 4 5 6 7 8 9 10 First Edition

One miserable and frozen spring

brisk brisk brisk

A cold little duck flew in

BRR-ACK BRR-ACK BRR-ACK

Her pond was stiff and white

creak creak creak

And her feet froze to the ice

stuck

stuck

stuck

stuck

You're
way too
early,
Duck,
go back
back
back

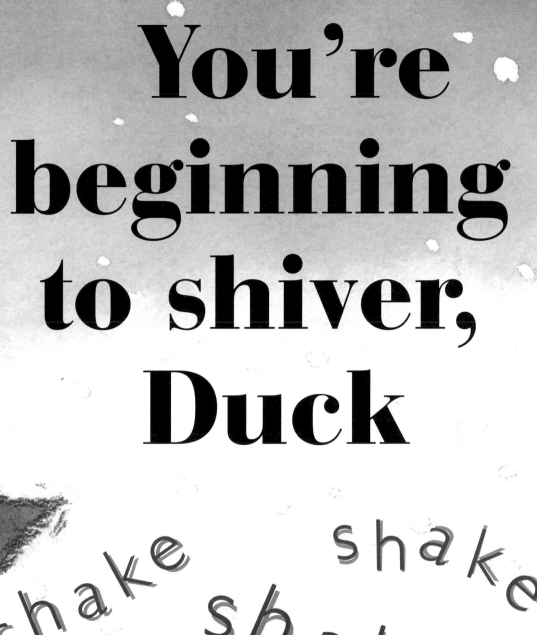

You're beginning to shiver, Duck

shake shake
shake shake

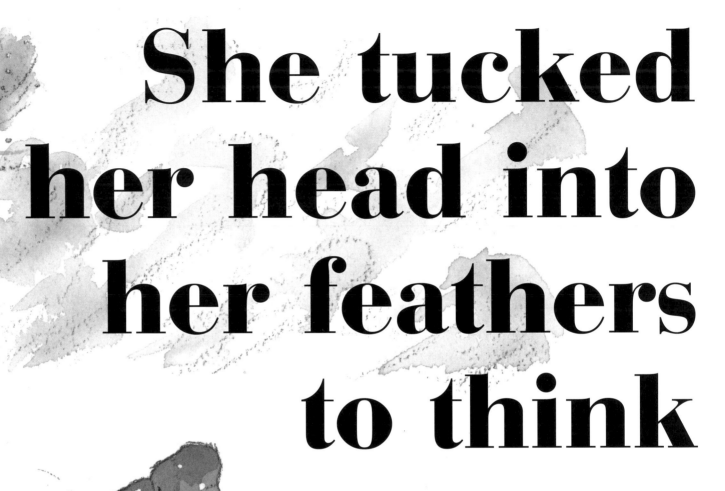

She tucked her head into her feathers to think

think think

Of spring and warmer weather

quick   quick   quick

Of
wiggly worms
and shiny
beetles

black

black

black

Of crocuses
and apple
buds

pink
pink pink

Her thoughts
of spring
filled the sky

thick

thick

thick

Until
a **V** of
ducks
flew
by

flock
flock
flock

They saw that spring was in the air

blink blink blink

The ducks flew down, they dipped and splashed

dunk
dunk
dunk

Come join us, Duck, it's melting fast

The cold little duck began to slide

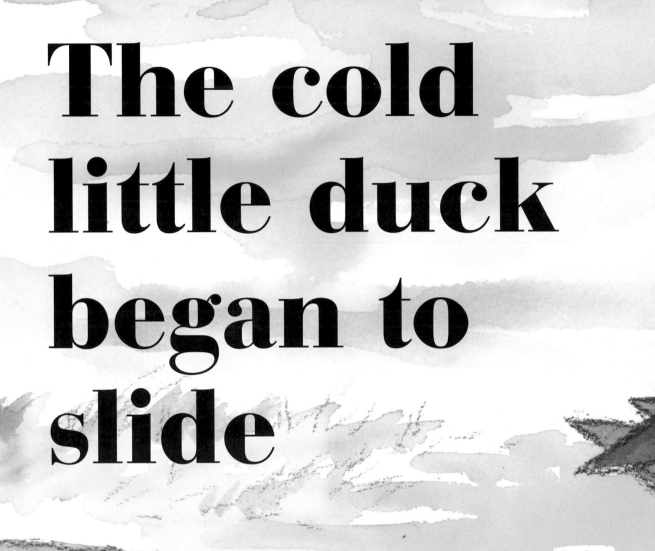

slick slick slick

Across the disappearing ice

CRACK
CRACK
CRRR . . . . ACK

She wiggled her tail, waggled her wings

kick
kick
kick

The warm little duck dove into spring

Quack

Quack